Vroom & Zoom

Written and illustrated by
Andrew Buller

The wise wind whistled...

www.meettherhymers.com
www.andrewbuller.com

Our red Rhymers have said,
"There are rhymes to be read."

The Rhymers - Collect them all

Vroom & Zoom
Nap & Yap
Izzy & Whizzy
Flex & X

Pop & Top
Mime & Rhyme
Hairy & Scary
Egg & Leg
Ace & Bass

Over & Under
Kick & Quick
Giggle & Jiggle
Crash & Dash

Andrew Buller Books

First published in Great Britain in 2015

ISBN: 978-1505263176

Vroom & Zoom

Written and illustrated by
Andrew Buller

The wise wind whistled...

www.meettherhymers.com
www.andrewbuller.com

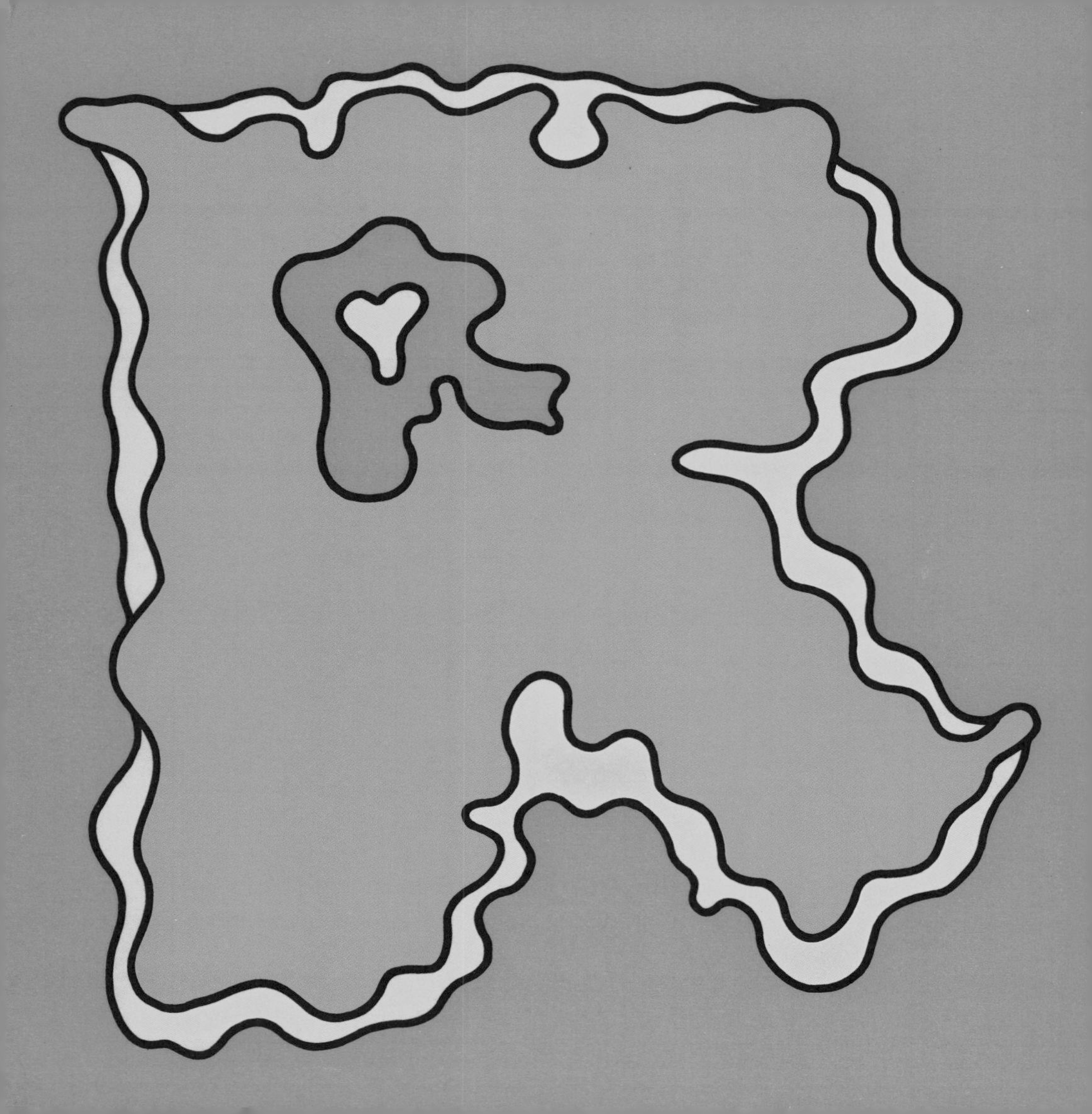

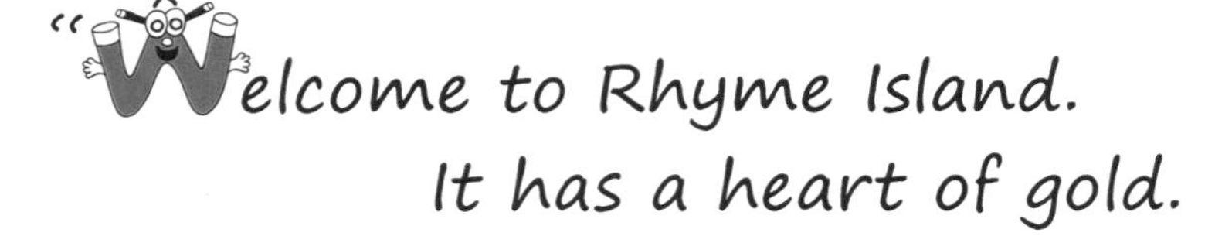

"Welcome to Rhyme Island.
It has a heart of gold.

We twenty six Rhymers live here
with stories to be told.

We join to make up every word.
We rhyme and sing and play.

Vroom and Zoom are waiting.
What will they do today?"

Zoom's tummy twitched.

He z-zz-**zoomed** quietly
from his alpha-bed,
trying not to wake Vroom.

But Vroom was awake.

"Now what,
oh what
are you
up to?"

It was still dark
when Zoom slid from Rocket Room.

His tummy knew where it was taking him.

"Z-zz-zoom."

Vroom followed as fast as he could.

"V-vv-vroom."

Zoom soared into the sky,
eating clouds as he flew by.

"A cloud of cheese, another of mash,
a milky cloud with a splash.
A banana cloud with a squirt of cream,
topped with chocolate,
such a cloud-feast dream.

My head's not sure
what I should do.
My twitchy tummy
wants something new."

Vroom tried his best to keep up
as Zoom left Rhyme Island far behind.

"Tummy take me
to where new tastes loom.
What I need
is that new tasty plume."

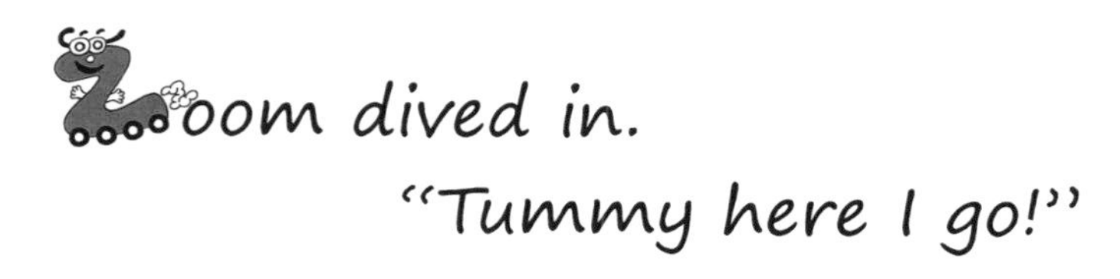

Zoom dived in.

"Tummy here I go!"

Vroom couldn't be heard crying, "No! No! No!"

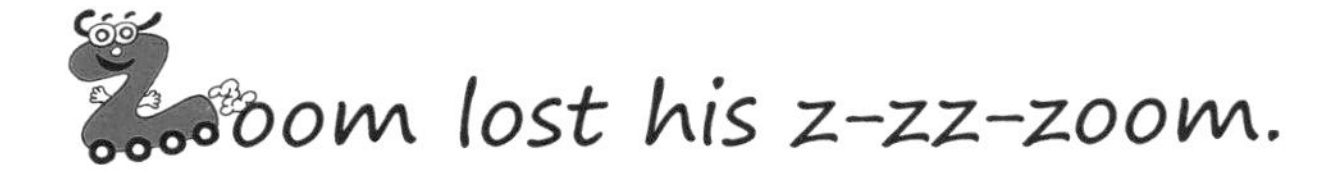

Zoom lost his z-zz-zoom.

He began to

fall,

fall,

fall.

"Oh, what a

fool,

fool,

fool!"

Vroom felt helpless.

"Rhyme Rescue!
Rhyme Rescue!
Please hear my call.

Please save my Rhymer from his fall,
fall,
fall!"

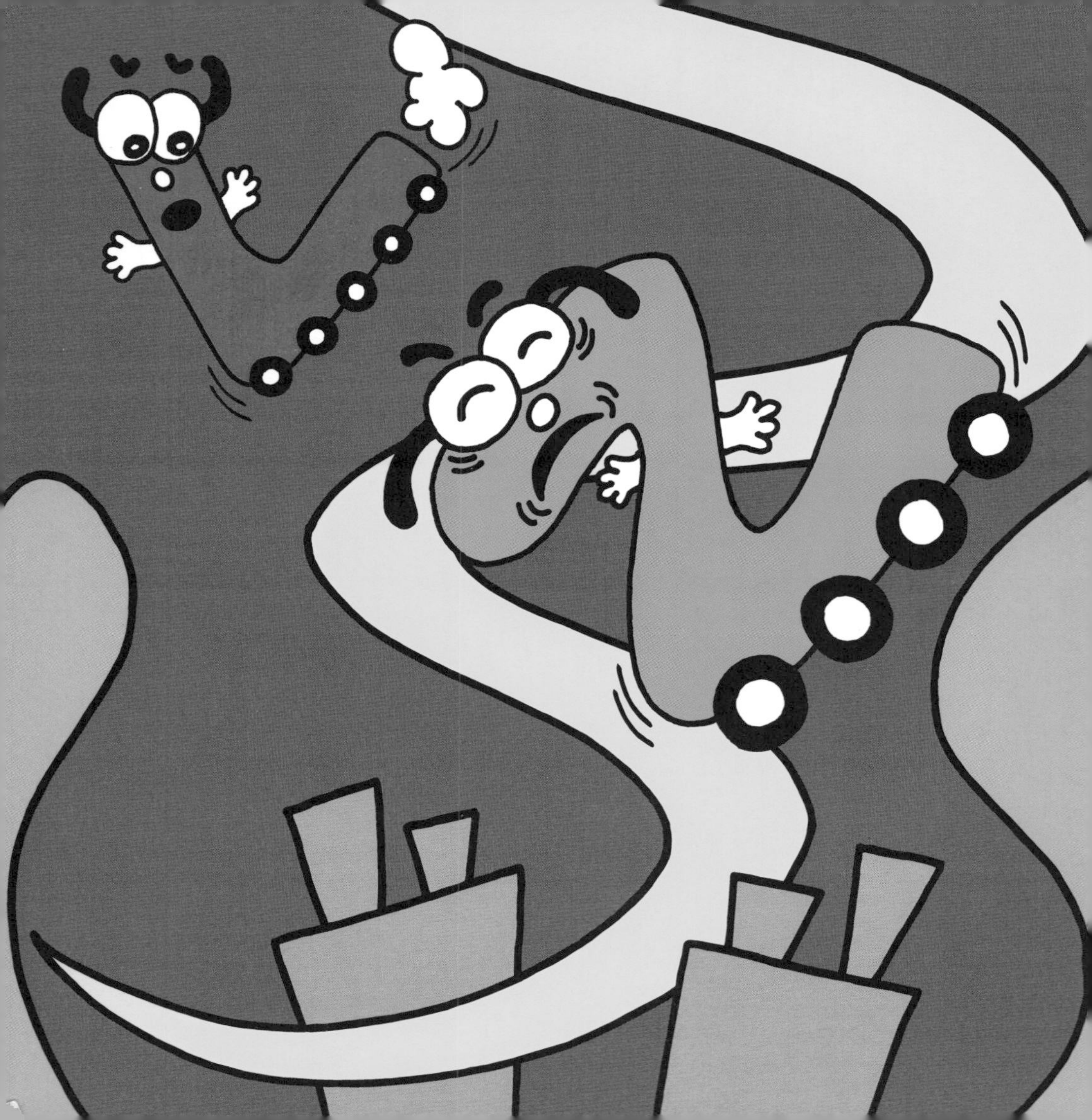

The wise wind whirled.

The wise wind twirled.

Vroom was gaining

as Zoom slowed

and swirled.

Vroom caught his Rhymer
just before he crashed.

"Let's get back to Rhyme Island.
It's time to streak and soar.
I need to fly faster
than I've ever vroomed before."

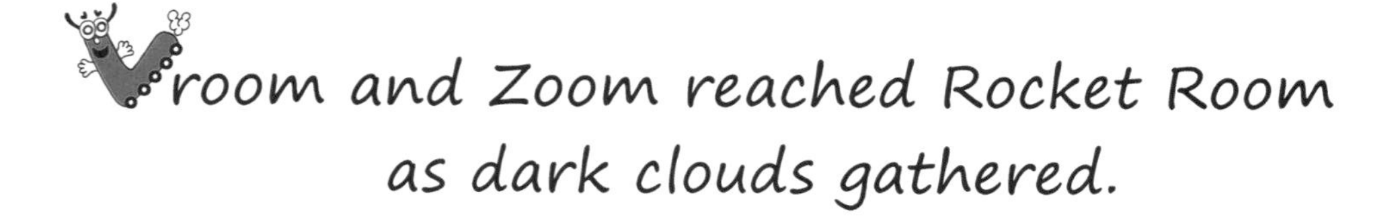

Vroom and Zoom reached Rocket Room
as dark clouds gathered.

All The Rhymers gathered too.

"Zoom is in trouble.
Big trouble!"

For two whole nights
and two whole days,
Zoom lay in his alpha-bed,
in a spinning haze.

His mind whirled, wildly,
his tummy was fizzing,
his alpha-bed was shaking
and his whole world whizzing.

Everyone waited.

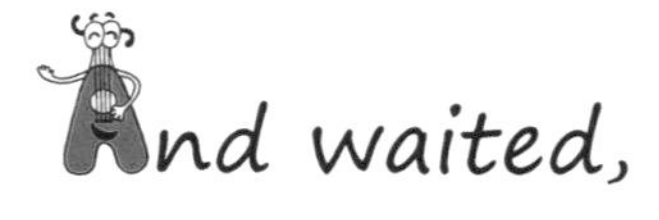

And waited,

and waited,

and waited.

Even the waiting waited.

hen,

early on the third morning,

came the loudest,

"BOOM-ZOOM"

ever heard.

Rocket Room shook.

Rhyme Island shook.

Even the sky shook.

Zoom shook,

sat up

and spoke.

"Pardon me.

That was loud.

What **did** they pump

into that cloud?"

Zoom climbed slowly from his bed,
"I need to see the sky."
He slid his way through parting clouds
and floated way up high.

He waved, he coughed, he looped the loop,
the Rhymers cheered brave Zoom.
"Don't cheer me, I'm not the star.
Come and join me Vroom!"

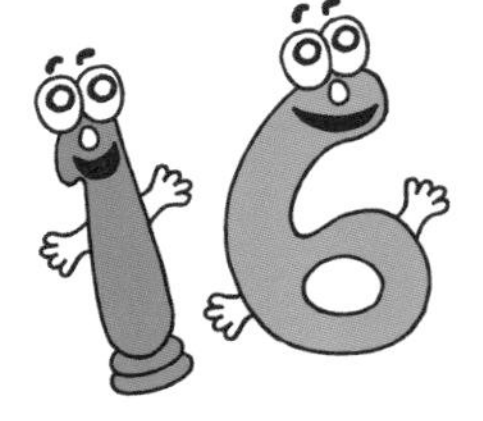

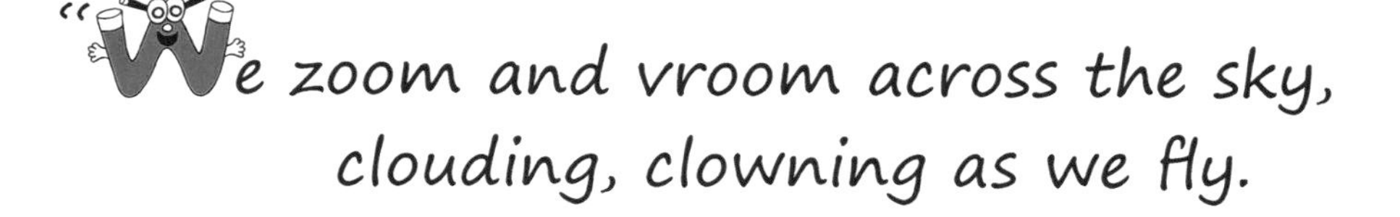

“We zoom and vroom across the sky,
clouding, clowning as we fly.

When we eat, huge bites we take.
We love the patterns that we make.

When you see pictures in the sky,
it’s just us, saying **Hi!**

When clouds dance round
the moon and sun,
it’s two happy Rhymers
just having fun.”

In the land where Zoom had eaten,

left behind was a hole,

a hole of hope.

Series available as published:

The Rhymers

Vroom & Zoom
Nap & Yap
Izzy & Whizzy
Flex & X

Pop & Top
Mime & Rhyme
Hairy & Scary
Egg & Leg
Ace & Bass

Over & Under
Kick & Quick
Giggle & Jiggle
Crash & Dash

Puzzling Rhymers

Vroom & Zoom
Nap & Yap
Izzy & Whizzy
Flex & X

Pop & Top
Mime & Rhyme
Hairy & Scary
Egg & Leg
Ace & Bass

Over & Under
Kick & Quick
Giggle & Jiggle
Crash & Dash

Colour Me Rhymers

Vroom & Zoom
Nap & Yap
Izzy & Whizzy
Flex & X

Pop & Top
Mime & Rhyme
Hairy & Scary
Egg & Leg
Ace & Bass

Over & Under
Kick & Quick
Giggle & Jiggle
Crash & Dash

The wise wind whistled...

www.meettherhymers.com

www.andrewbuller.com

Dear Oz,

Thank you so much for all your support, encouragement, friendship and prayers.

I hope you enjoy my first book!! ;)

God bless you and your family.

Andrew

Made in the USA
Charleston, SC
04 February 2015